D1551231

The

ᛑDON CE-SAR

STORY

By June Hurley Young

ISBN 0-941072-21-5

PARTNERSHIP PRESS

Other Books By June Hurley Young

How to Be Your Child's Best Teacher 1980
Florida's Pinellas Peninsula 1983
Reprinted 2000
The Vinoy....Faded Glory Renewed 1998
Don't Tell Me I Can't Do It 2007

THE DON CESAR STORY
Seventh Printing 2013
Sixth Printing 2007
Fifth Printing 1997
Fourth Printing 1987
Third Printing 1978
Second Printing 1975
Copyright By June Hurley 1974

PARTNERSHIP PRESS
362 89th AveNE
St. Petersburg, Florida 33702

TABLE OF CONTENTS

Introduction

The story of the Don Ce-Sar Hotel in St. Petersburg Beach, Florida, is a series of mountains and valleys. For a while things go well. Then something happens. The economy nosedives, the owner dies, a project is abandoned and everyone moves out. Then, much like the legendary Don Caesar DeBazan for whom the building was named, there's a sudden reprieve, a new life, and the Don blossoms for another era of usefulness.

Don Caesar is the hero of Vincent Wallace's opera "Maritana." In the story he is sentenced by Spain's King Charles II to be executed by a firing squad. But the guns misfire. The smoke clears, and the Don stands unharmed. Miraculously he is saved and pardoned. Similarly the Don Ce-Sar Hotel seems to lead an equally charmed life. Wrecking crews were about to destroy the building in 1971 when local citizens fought to save it.

This book is more than just the story of a well-known landmark. It's a testimony to the reader that persistence pays. The amazing rebirth of the discarded Don was the work of many. Together they proved the efficacy of that famous passage from Romans, "All things work together for good."

I hope that this proof of victory will be assurance to you, the reader, that you, too, can achieve a goal when you believe in your success and you persist.

I want to thank all those who helped me assemble this historical book; Frank Hurley for his assistance; and the rest of my family and friends who listened with understanding and encouraged me throughout the three years that I was involved in brainstorming and publicizing the Don Ce-Sar Hotel.

June Hurley Young

THOMAS J. ROWE

Chapter I

THE MAKING OF A MILLIONAIRE

A mysterious charisma clings to the Don Ce-Sar, giving it a unique personality, forging an almost supernatural link with its indomitable builder, Thomas J. Rowe.

At age 42, Rowe left his wife in Norfolk, Virginia and came to St. Petersburg. He looked as if he were in his late 50's, broken in health and spirit, and with very little money to invest. Born in Boston, he was orphaned at the age of 4. He was sent back to his grandfather who was still in Ireland. Educated in England he returned to the United States when he was 18 and he settled in Virginia where he was a real estate broker. A severe heart condition and asthma ended his career and sent him to Florida.

Shortly after arriving in town, he started out one day to look over some property with Fred Sumner, a local broker. On their way to the West Central area they crossed a rough spot on Central Avenue near 15th Street where the road dipped to an old wooden bridge over Booker Creek. Sumner took the dip too fast, throwing Rowe against the top of the car and cutting his head.

Instead of showing the property, he apologetically hurried Rowe to a doctor, then back to his hotel. Rowe refused to go with him again, saying, "A man who drives like that can't be trusted as a broker!"

It was probably that cut on his head which caused him to inquire at Walter Fuller's real estate office later that day. It began a relationship which changed the fortunes of both visionaries.

1

Fifty-four years later, Fuller still remembered their first meeting. He was checking his listings in a "cubbyhole" office at 5th and Central on a sultry spring day in 1919 when Rowe, bareheaded and with a cut over his eyebrow, greeted him through the open door.

"Show me the best speculative buy in St. Petersburg," he challenged.

Fuller named a piece of land at 11th and Central which was listed for $800.

"Now, Mr. Fuller, I'm going to make you an unusual proposition. You can't collect a commission for buying me something, but I'll pay you double the commission when you sell it for me."

Fuller, realizing there was no way he could lose, agreed. He bought the land for Rowe for $800, sold it a few weeks later for $1,100 and was paid his $110 commission.

Pleased with their initial transaction, Rowe turned over his total assets of $10,000 cash and an $11,000 mortgage to Fuller, giving him full authority to buy and sell for him.

At that time Rowe lived alone in a hotel on Second Street. He was so sick most of the time that he left all details of his real estate transactions to his energetic young broker until the day he heard that Perry Snell's 80-acre tract of land north of Pass-a-Grille Beach could be bought for $100,000. This land today is the part of St. Petersburg Beach between 30th and 35th Avenues.

For some reason, the island fascinated him. He rushed to Fuller's office. "Walter, buy that land!" he ordered.

Fuller couldn't believe Rowe was serious. He was against the move and outlined his objections in no uncertain terms.

"The only access to the island is McAdoo's frail, wooden toll bridge which he operates, according to his whim, usually from 6 a.m. to 9 p.m. daily. You'd be at his mercy. And once you're on the island, the only way to reach Pass-a-Grille is by a rough nine-foot brick road. If you're thinking of going into the hotel business there, you'll undoubtedly lose money."

"You're a sick man, Tom, the worry of a development like that could kill you. Besides, both of us know that the boom's liable to blow up any minute."

Nothing could dissuade Rowe. Several days later he returned to ask if Fuller had closed the deal. Again he sternly ordered, "Walter, buy that land or I will."

When Fuller again refused, Rowe closed the purchase himself. It was the first rift between the two. Rowe walked stiffly into his friend's office, requested a statement of his assets and a final settlement, less the commission.

"I was heartbroken to end our relationship," remembered Fuller. "I handed him his statement and a check and mortgages totaling $1,050,000. It was all earned from his $21,000 capital in a few months less than six years."

The groundwork was laid. Thomas Rowe had his island paradise and grandiose plans for creating a magnificent subdivision of Spanish-style estates. He would crown his beach retreat with the castle-like hotel he visualized. Perhaps his plans were 50 years before their time, but this intuitive man was impatient and knew that he must work fast to realize the dream within his lifetime.

His destiny as a famous Florida developer was soon to take a new road without Walter Fuller, his friend and financial advisor. Rowe seemed to be able to predict the future. He, too, sensed the approaching end of the boom. Perhaps risking a fortune to develop a little-known island was his "leap of faith," his way of saying to fellow investors, "Look at me. If I'm willing to risk it, why shouldn't you? We may keep the bottom from dropping out by building with optimism."

It may have been financial foresight or it may have been his all-consuming desire to put money into his "monument" which prompted him to discount mortgages which he held and gather all the cash possible before the boom collapsed. In any event, by July 1925 he had sold most lots in his subdivision at the prevailing high price of $5,000. Some sold for cash but many for one-third cash with the balance payable monthly. Gathering in his funds, Rowe wrote to property owners in his subdivision telling them he thought his prices were too high and that he'd give them a 33-1/3% discount if they paid off their mortgages immediately.

His vision saved him while less foresighted developers lost everything. And, when the boom blew up in 1926, he was already building the Don Ce-Sar. He sent for his old friend Fuller and advised him of the financial storm brewing. He gave him $5,000, "not as a loan, but as a gift, saying, 'Don't come and ask me for any more help because I can't give it to you.' "

Just weeks before Fuller died in November, 1973, he fondly reminisced, saying, "We only had one dispute and that was over buying the Don Ce-Sar property. He was a great man, a good man, yes, and a stubborn man, too. He never bought a piece of real estate on which he didn't make a profit. He was the smartest real estate man this area has ever known."

1925   Aerial view looking East at Rowe's land surrounding Don Ce-Sar Bay.   Current site of the Bayway Bridge.

Chapter II

BUILDING   A   DREAM

Thomas Rowe was filled with pride and anticipation when he first surveyed his private stretch of island. The lush tropical foliage, sun-drenched beach and sparkling surf reminded him of the natural beauty he'd seen on a trip to Hawaii.

With his Irish flair for the romantic, he could visualize a great hotel like Waikiki Beach's Royal Hawaiian framed against the rich blue Florida sky. He saw curved boulevards with formal rows of palm trees, oleanders and cork trees, and fine homes rising from the jungle wilderness.

Rowe was realistic enough, though, to heed Fuller's warning. McAdoo's bridge was too precarious and the unstable, single-lane brick road running the length of Long Key was at times almost impassable. Trucks heavily laden with building materials could never make it under such poor conditions.

5

One of the barges used for transporting all the construction materials.

There was, however, ample access to his property by water. He determined that the shallow bay could accommodate small barges and so that would be his mode of transportation.

It was 1925. In St. Petersburg the boom was going strong and a record number of building permits had been issued. Many of the major hotels still standing today were under construction — the Soreno, Pheil, Suwannee, Mason (now the Princess Martha), Pennsylvania, Dennis, Rolyat (now Stetson Law School), and the Jungle Country Club (now Admiral Farragut Academy). Although good workmen were scarce and much in demand, Rowe found them and began to make his dream a reality.

No detail escaped his attention. He subdivided his 80 acres into lots and began building Spanish-style houses. The deed restrictions which he placed on the property are still in effect today. He guaranteed residents access to the valuable beach frontage, reserving two blocks solely for them. Parks were designated, and much of the land restricted to single family dwellings.

Then, from his first office at 15th and Central Avenue in St. Petersburg, he and his contractor, Carlton Beard, turned their attention to the castle-like hotel that would crown the perfect subdivision. Henry Dupont, a well-known Indianapolis architect, accepted the commission to design the building and moved his firm to St. Petersburg.

With a romantic flair, Rowe chose names for his hotel and his community from his favorite American opera "Maritana". He changed Don Caesar the leading character's name to Don Ce-Sar. The original plans for his grand hotel were for a $450,000 "T" shaped, six-story building with 110 rooms and baths. However, it wasn't long after construction began that Rowe decided to enlarge the hotel to ten-stories and 220 rooms and 220 baths. This boosted the cost to $650,000.

Local builders shook their heads pessimistically. "How can you build a heavy structure like that on shifting beach sand?" they muttered skeptically. "Can you imagine the cost of sinking pilings to insure a solid foundation?"

However, the ingenious Carlton Beard devised a floating pad of concrete and pyramided footings, the same type of foundation used in constructing Mexico City over a lake.

Beard experimented for two weeks and made tests. The concrete hadn't settled an eighth of an inch. Forty-five years later, there is still no settling evident in any part of the building.

Three stepped slabs of cement two feet thick were poured as footings for the foundation and the slow process of raising a monolithic giant in the wilderness began.

Among the sand and palmettoes Beard rigged a 185-foot tower and a hopper to carry the cement mixture. Using a primitive dump and chute method,

Pouring slabs and uprights was a slow, tedious process.

workmen cast the uprights. Building a skyscraper this way was slow and agonizing. Today a skeleton for such a building could be poured in less than a week. Then it took many months.

The Belgian cement and gravel brought in on the barges was mixed with beach sand and reinforced with heavy twisted iron rods.

By selling 900 acres of land held elsewhere in Pinellas County, Rowe had $900,000 cash which he deposited in Central Bank. But by early 1926, the boom was over. Rowe's funds were tied up in land, and he had to depend on time payments sent him in the mail to meet his payroll and building supply bills.

Walter Gregory, former president of Pinellas Lumber Company, sold Rowe most of his supplies and was always promptly paid. "Those were hard times — many developers lost all they had," he remembers. "Thomas

Rowe was one man in a thousand, a fine gentleman. Nothing stopped him. He was determined to finish his hotel and kept doggedly on."

When money was low and work halted on the Don, Rowe would invite Beard to take a drive to Miami in his Marmon roadster. They would confer with east coast architects and buy plans for Spanish houses. "He never let me hear the last of it, the time I paid $200 for three sets of plans," remembers Beard.

The architecture of the Don Ce-Sar became a blend of the Mediterrannean and Moorish themes the two men admired on the East Coast. They were influenced by James Deering's Vizcaya, George Merrick's Coral Gables development and Addison Mizner's work in Boca Raton and in Palm Beach.

Stucco over hollow tile, red clay tile roofs, arched openings, balconies and tower-like upper stories were touches they borrowed. Later, Wade Callahan actually designed the towers, ornamental boxes, swags, urns and borders to frost the hotel's facade.

"The hotel, the way Dupont planned it, was something of a Plain Jane," says Beard. "Mr. Rowe was becoming dissatisfied with the first plans and revisions. When he discovered that Dupont made no provision for entering the hotel except by a dark, narrow back stairway, he fired him."

Rowe and Beard took over the planning and the building of the Don Ce-Sar and worked the way Addison Mizner worked, "Construction first, blueprints afterward." Craftsmen worked from sketches and on-the-spot instructions. Foremost in Rowe's mind was that he wanted a sweeping staircase in the style of the European grand hotel.

He also decided to move his dining room to the top floor. These two revisions created a lobby floor of spacious public rooms. In order to create enough hotel rooms to make it pay, two more wings had to be added and costs soared again.

Construction as it was viewed from Maritana Drive (the portion now covered by the overpass).

Adding the towers gave the hotel its castle-like silhouette.

10

Unfortunately, Rowe was also plagued by problems with the Internal Revenue Service. They assumed he had actually collected the full price for lots he'd sold on time. To add to his dilemma, in 1926 and 1927 most buyers quit making payments.

Walter Bennett remembers lending him ten dollars. "I'm going to see my banker at Central Bank (now Union Trust)," Rowe told him. "I need a shave, haircut and a fresh carnation in my buttonhole when I ask for a loan."

All revisions and additions were so costly that from the original estimate of $450,000, costs rose to a staggering $1,250,000. All of Rowe's capital was exhausted. In desperation, he sought an angel to bail him out.

Warren Webster, a New Jersey industrialist, became Rowe's close friend. Caught up in his contagious enthusiasm for the Don Ce-Sar, he lent him enough money to furnish the hotel and took a mortgage on the property. It was this money which paid for the Oriental rugs, mahogany furniture, Black Knight china made especially in Germany for the hotel, and the finest horse-hair mattresses.

In the rush to finish the hotel, two carloads of expensive oak flooring were laid in the ballroom. There wasn't time for the adhesive to dry. To hurry it up, Rowe turned the steam heat all the way up, and the beautiful floor was "washboarded."

Frantically, he called his friend Walter Gregory for advice. "Resand and varnish the floor again," said Gregory. By opening night, the ripple in the floor was almost unnoticeable. The wood has never been removed and is part of the present ballroom dance floor.

At last, Rowe completed "The Mighty Don Ce-Sar." He sat back and surveyed his work of three years. Its bright spires pierced the island foliage, offering a beacon to sailors looking for a safe port in a storm. Beside the door he placed symbols of strength and stability, a pair of lions, a medallion of a ship, and a medallion of a

"The Mighty Don Ce-Sar" realization of Thomas Rowe's
dream was completed, December 1927.

compass. Over the door his greeting to his guests was
carved in stone: "Come all ye who seek health and rest,
for here they are abundant."

He was a proud, happy man that December 1927.
During his years since his arrival in Florida, he had
overcome poor health. He came as an invalid, an
asthmatic with a weak heart. Here he had found a new
life. He had realized his dream to build a monument to
the many blessings of health, wealth and peace of mind
that came to him since he had made his home on the
island.

In a tribute, he wrote: "The shores of heaven on the
Island of Pass-a-Grille where glory meets glory in the
rising and the setting sun." His motto, "Omne Solum
Forti, Patria Est: (Sun Is The Strengthening Father)
was inscribed on stationery and hotel furnishings.

His dream hotel, the Don Ce-Sar, was ready and he
would share its magic with all who came.

Chapter III

A NIGHT TO REMEMBER

All that first week of the new year, Carlton Beard and his crew were adding final touches. Nurserymen hurriedly planted a grove of palms in the park and the miniature golf course across Gulf Boulevard from the hotel was almost but not quite ready.

Ethel Fogg answered the phone. It was good news. The final load of furniture had arrived in St. Petersburg on the afternoon train. She quickly arranged for truckers to pick it up. For the past month since she'd come to work for Thomas Rowe, she had taken care of the many letters and the other last minute details involved in completing and opening "The Mighty Don Ce-Sar."

Actually, only 150 of the 300 rooms were scheduled for completion by opening day. The north wing, only partially finished, would be used to house the hotel staff for everyone would live on the premises during the season.

On January 10th, six days before opening, Thomas Wiles and his wife arrived from Boston to make history as the first guests to sign the register. They brought their maid with them and they all settled comfortably in a Gulf-front suite to watch the pageant of a large hotel opening.

Finally, on Monday, January 16, 1928, a full page ad in The St. Petersburg Times proclaimed: "Hurling Its Beauty to the Sky, This Castle-like Hostelry on the Shores of the Gulf Thrills You with its Grandeur."

Lights blazed in the high-arched windows, flowers filled the rooms, and 1,500 guests dined on the fifth floor and danced in the grand ballroom.

The dinner prepared by Chef White and dancing cost $2.50 per person. Beautifully gowned women and tuxedoed men from Tampa and St. Petersburg drove up to the red canopied entrance in La Salles, Chryslers,

13

Marmons and other limousines of that era. They toured the rooms and roof gardens at sunset, surveyed the rooms with private baths and exclaimed over the "magnificent view." They dined and danced to the music of the Don Ce-Sar orchestra and listened to the Brahms duet sung by Nella Erickson and Helen Ford.

The man of the hour, of course, was Thomas Rowe, a dapper, silver-haired man in a black suit. He smoked his cheroot and beamed happily as he acknowledged the congratulations of the admiring crowd. It was a night he'd never forget — the realization of years of hard work driven by his obsession to build the finest hotel on Florida's West Coast. The Don Ce-Sar was everything and more than he'd visualized, a self-contained resort community, away from it all, where wealthy businessmen could find the solitude they were seeking.

A week of parties celebrated the opening. Guests for the season arrived and Rowe enjoyed playing host that January and February. He never believed in advertising. The next year others came on the recommendation of satisfied friends.

Because Warren Webster had invested in the Don's future, he helped select the first manager, H.B. Churchill. Mrs. Churchill handled all the banquet and party details, coordinating even flowers and place cards.

Barbara Plank remembers working with her mother in the ground floor gift shop where guests enjoyed gathering. Her father operated the newstand on the same floor near the stairs to the lobby. Someone had to make the daily trip into St. Petersburg for film and stamps for his stand, and fresh flowers for the florist.

Also on the ground floor was Anne Gunter's Beauty Shop. She started a tradition by giving every little boy his first haircut for a penny. Mrs. Paul White was one of the mothers who remembers taking her young son to Anne.

In those early days, Jean Renwick was Thomas Rowe's "girl Friday." Everywhere at once, she paid Carlton Beard, mimeographed menus, answered letters and even sang at evening musicals. She opened employment applications. Young Art Feidt wrote from Toledo. She remembers he was hired that year as desk clerk; someday he would become manager.

Thomas Rowe often procrastinated answering mail until minutes before quitting time, remembers his private secretary, Lucille Wilson. "He'd save the letters and bring them to me just before noon Saturday morning."

Two hundred staff members pampered one hundred guests. There were balls, golfing tournaments in Pasadena, horseback riding, fashion shows and entertainments. Even Sally Rand did her famous fan dance in the ballroom.

Rowe presided like the lord of the manor from his high-backed chair at the top of the stairs. His staff was "his family." He would ask a guest to leave if they mistreated one of the help, saying, "I have to depend on these people to keep things going at my hotel. I will not have them offended." People were always important to him. If a guest was sick, he'd ask resident nurse Mary Berg about his health and stop by daily to cheer him up.

His daily ritual included dressing in a neat, conservative suit, ordering his Marmon and driving around his subdivision. Rowe waved to all the property owners as he drove by as though they were his loyal subjects. His whole life was Don Ce-Sar, his community and his hotel.

Chapter IV

CASTLE IN THE WILDERNESS

The Don Ce-Sar was a rosy spot in the blue and green island wilderness. Rowe would tell you its color was "rouge;" reminiscent of the rosy lime mixed with mortar that he saw in Ireland when he was a child. He found the right mixture and copied it to stucco the hotel's exterior.

Red tile roofs gave the building a Spanish solidity. The six towers added to the hotel's majestic appearance. No one realized that they were as practical as they were artistic, for one camouflaged the chimney and another held the large pressure water tank. The island's frail water system was so inadequate that many beach residents couldn't get water on the second floor of their homes, but Rowe had to have enough water pressure to serve all ten stories of his building.

Through many-paned fan-shaped windows, sunshine streamed in, illuminating the grand ballroom, lobby and writing room, the immense dining room and all the guest rooms. Every room seemed "as big as the whole outdoors," for everywhere there was a view of the Gulf or Bay.

Inside, the Don Ce-Sar was almost austere in its simplicity. There was quiet strength and permanence in the heavy Doric pillars. Cream walls were a background for high-backed mahogany chairs covered in wine cut velvet. Rowe's one concession to elegance was the heavy dark red velvet draping the windows, although he revolted against 19th century Victorian frills. His masculine taste and the stark 30's set the trend.

16

The lobby was typical of the formal elegance of the 30's. Today only a third of this area is used as a passageway to the Grand Ballroom. The rest is divided into private rooms, the Bar De Bazan, and the Coffee Shop.

Every window was covered with Venetian blinds, the newest fad of this era.

Highly-polished oak floors were centered with dark Oriental rugs. The sun room on the Gulf was furnished with white wicker furniture and had a Spanish fountain in the center.

The cavernous fifth floor was divided into dining room and kitchen. It was floored with inlaid broken Spanish tile. Small bronze fixtures on the ceiling illuminated every table, white bronze scounces lighted the walls. Each table was set with white linen, sparkling crystal, the formal Black Knight china and a brigade of silver flatware.

Guests had a regular table overlooking the Gulf. The staff ate in the large part of the dining room that over-looked Don Ce-Sar community. (As the years passed, Rowe was always building partitions and rearranging furniture to break up the enormous expanse of dining room, but his efforts were never successful. His staff said the walls he put up one season would be torn down the next).

The kitchen occupying the entire north wing was so immense that the help had to make many steps in the preparation and serving of meals. Since this was the only kitchen, food had to be transported by elevator to serve the ballroom or the beach.

Although there were many suites on each floor, the majority of the guest rooms were single rooms with adjoining baths. Each was furnished with painted metal twin beds with springs and horsehair mattresses, a mahogany writing desk, two chairs, tailored bedspreads, velvet draperies and an Oriental rug. At the entrance way, there was a closet on one side and a white tiled bath on the other. The Don was one of the first hotels to have heavy built-in porcelain bath tubs. The plumbing was all cast iron and easily accessible because the practical builder left chases that opened onto the hallway.

Rooms were high-ceilinged and cool, but this was of little importance then since the hotel was only open from January through February. However, the Don's unique location between Bay and Gulf took advantage of nature's cooling system. Sea breezes hit the face of the building and eddied around the sides, cooling the interiors. There was always the Bay breeze in the morning that kept things cool until the wind swung around to the west in the afternoon and reversed the cycle.

On the ground floor was a wine cellar, pantry, a boiler room, storage facilities, the children's dining room and the entrance-way to the beach.

Gulfside verandas were a new concept for resort-goers. Everyone dressed so formally that the idea of sun-bathing was unheard of then. Even at the beach women wore bathing dresses and stockings and men wore tops with their swim trunks. Rowe believed his guests should discover a new way of life as they basked in the sunshine so he included sun-drenched verandas bordering the grand staircase. This was another Don Ce-Sar first.

On the beach, the men lounged in white flannel trousers and sports jackets; the women wore pastel dresses and wide-brimmed hats. It was a picture out of an F. Scott Fitzgerald novel.

January and February of 1929, the Don Ce-Sar was filled to capacity. Many of the country's wealthiest families played under the Florida sun, oblivious to storm clouds gathering over Wall Street.

Chapter V

THE LEAN HARD YEARS

merica's post-war prosperity ended abruptly on October 29, 1929. Tremors from the Stock Market Crash shook the nation's economy, threatening the future of the Don Ce-Sar.

In addition to his mortgage to Warren Webster, Rowe had floated a half-million dollar bond issue to finish the hotel. During the Depression, he couldn't meet payments. The hotel was thrown into receivership.

Judge Frank Hobson held the hearing. Warren Webster and Erle Askew were instrumental in having Rowe appointed receiver. Instead of losing the hotel, he was given an opportunity to keep it open and try to work it out of debt. The investors also had a chance of someday getting their money back.

"It was a surprisingly good season in 1930," said Art Feidt. "We began receiving reservations from wealthy Jewish families, the department store tycoons — Pogue, Bloomingdale, Gimbel, Lazarus, Feiner of the May Company of St. Louis, Mrs. Caesar Cone Mills of Greensboro, Isaac Liberman of Arnold Constable in New York, and Herb Steiner of Jean Nate.

Also in 1930 the famous writer, F. Scott Fitzgerald brought his lovely wife Zelda to the hotel for the season. When he asked Rowe's secretary to help him, the staff started the rumor that he was writing a mystery story about the Don Ce-Sar. She took down 50 answers to fan letters while he paced back and forth in his suite.

In several books, Fitzgerald mentioned "the hotel in an island wilderness." His fondness for the peaceful isolation he treasured is mirrored in *Crack-Up*: "We went to Florida. The bleak marshes were punctuated by Biblical admonitions to a better life; abandoned fishing boats disintegrated in the sun. The Don Ce-Sar Hotel in Pass-a-Grille stretched lazily over the stubbed wilderness, surrendering its shape to the blinding brightness of the gulf," he wrote.

The Soreno and Vinoy hotels in St. Petersburg capitalized on the Don's picturesque location by advertising they had a Gulf beach. They paid twenty-five cents per person and transported their guests out to use the Don's beach.

Rates at the Don Ce-Sar were $24 per day double or $30 for a suite, $12 or $14 for single rooms and all rates included meals.

At Saturday night dinner dances, sons of prominent "in town" families were invited to escort the daughters of the wealthy guests. Most of the boys were pretty unhappy about this situation until the night they caught an alligator in the road on the way home. "At least that night wasn't an entire waste!" said one.

Mary Hastings Christensen , then a young nurse-companion to the aging Mrs. Warren Webster, remembers those gala Saturday night balls. After dressing in a new gown, she'd stop at the beauty shop where Anne Gunter would decorate her hair with sequins and plumes for the party.

The Squires, the Dragons and other St. Petersburg social clubs held balls at the Don. Mrs. Bill Bond recalls dancing with her sweetheart, Bill, at her St. Petersburg High School Prom. Bill, of course, was the Bill Bond she later married.

At the end of the 1930 season, Rowe was able to bank $84,000 in the Central Bank after expenses and taxes. Unfortunately, the bank failed in the Spring of 1931. His savings disappeared and Rowe had nothing left to finance the next season.

It was probably the three-year contract to house the New York Yankees that saved the hotel. Colonel Jacob Ruppert, the Yankee's owner, Joe McCarthy, the team manager, and Mark Roth, road secretary, were familiar faces around the Don. The team attracted a satellite of sports writers and family members, so the hotel was well-filled with 125 rooms sold out for the season. By this time, rates were down to $8 per person, double occupancy, including meals.

One stipulation was that players would be served steak every morning at breakfast as well as unlimited quantities of milk. All Yankees, except Babe Ruth, were quartered in the hotel. It was Col. Ruppert's way of getting the men away from the "flesh pots" of St. Petersburg.

Lou Gehrig, Babe Ruth, Bill Dickey, Lefty Gomez, Tony Lazzari, Red Ruffing and Frank Crosetti were among the Yankees who signed a souvenir baseball for secretary Irene Heinous that year at the Don.

Rowe was dismayed at the change in his hotel's clientele. He continued, nevertheless, to demand that dignity be maintained at all times. Everyone, including the staff, always dressed for dinner and coats and ties were always worn in the lobby.

One day sports writer Bill Corum was in the lobby sending a telegram. Rowe came up the grand staircase, surveyed the scene and spotted Corum wearing a hat. He walked up, tapped Corum on the shoulder and said, "Take off your hat." The writer stared back uncomprehendingly. "I said, TAKE OFF YOUR HAT! You can't wear a hat in MY lobby," Rowe shouted. He never relaxed his principles.

Even with the hotel nearly empty he never hesitated to ask guests to leave if their conduct was unacceptable. One such case involved a woman who had been sitting at the other end of the lobby knitting too loudly.

The Don's miniature golf course, on the lot across Gulf Boulevard, was the finest in the South, but the guests couldn't use it for a long time. The sheltering palms attracted clouds of sand flies and mosquitoes. Rowe used his own money to start Pinellas County's first Mosquito Control Board which he headed until his death. Claude Strickland said, "Rowe was more careful about spending the Board's money than he was his own."

In 1933, one guest, a Mr. Coombs, warned Rowe to take his money out of the banks. Secretively, Coombs cashed a big check everyday at the hotel and then had the cash (it soon amounted to $50,000) put in the hotel's safe. Unfortunately, Rowe didn't listen to the man's good advice. Maybe it was because he hoped his optimism and confidence would assure others to leave their money in the bank and thus avert complete financial disaster.

In any event, banks closed. Rowe, along with everyone else, was dealt another staggering blow. People had no money to buy gas. The hotel had only $100 in the cash register. Travelers checks had to be cashed downtown.

There was virtually no business. "I can't afford to pay you," Rowe sadly told his staff in 1934.

By late January, there were only eight guests in the house. "I have to cut your salary in half," he apologized to the staff. "When we get to the end of the year, I'll see if I can make it up to you."

At the end of the season, after paying the bills, Rowe gave his workers every penny they had coming in back pay. "I'm so glad I could do it. I was worried about doing that to you," he told them.

Art Feidt said, "The guy was admirable. I loved him. He was like a father to me. He had great vision —— 50 years ahead of himself —— impatient —— one of the dreamers like Flagler and Plant. He put down his last dime for his dream. Some say it killed him. I think it kept him alive."

Somehow the Don Ce-Sar survived those hectic years and Rowe, as owner-manager from 1932 to 1940, worked relentlessly until his hotel was finally debt-free.

One innovation of this period was a ground-floor "beverage room." Rowe detested drinking, but, after Prohibition, bowed to the wishes of his more influential guests. Leon Ott was the only bartender who managed to make the bar pay, yet Rowe never allowed drinking above the ground level.

Once a local family took a bottle to a Dragon Club dance. Because of Rowe's rules, they smuggled it in

Barbara Plank (third from the left) modeled in a Beach-wear Show, one of the hotel's entertainments for guests in the 1930's.

wrapped in the wife's fur coat. Someone asked her to dance. She forgot she had the bottle and got up. To her dismay and embarrassment, it fell and smashed on the ballroom floor.

One of the greatest pleasures of the guests was having lunch on the beach. For twenty-five cents, a waiter set up an umbrella and table, carried the food down from the fifth floor and served it. One doctor complained every month and refused to pay the twenty-five cent service charges on his bill.

Many staff members made lasting friendships and received fine gifts from wealthy guests — like the $50 alligator bag Dr. Bernheim sent each secretary. But, on the other extreme was the penny-pincher who took free oranges from a box in the hallway, saved them up and left them on her dresser as a tip for the maids.

In the mid and late 1930's, the register was filled with the names of famous guests; J. Montgomery Flagg, illustrator; Henry King, movie director; David Bernstein, vice president of MGM; Mignon Eberhardt, mystery writer; Faith Baldwin, novelist; Clarence Darrow,

24

attorney of the famous Scopes monkey trial; and Henry Doherty of Cities Service.

The pages looked like something out of *Who's Who In America*. They included the signatures of Charles Kidder, Henry Morgenthau's mother, Robert Scott of Waterman Pen; Tom Girdler of Republic Steel; John Boyd Thatcher, Mayor of Albany, N.Y., a power in the Democratic party and friend of Al Smith and Franklin Delano Roosevelt.

Sometimes in the midst of the opulent guests there would be hard-looking men with broad-brimmed hats and bulges under their coats. Many were said to be associated with notorious gangland figures.

Cashier Jean Renwick Ott thinks, "The gangsters came here because they thought it was a good hideout away from everything."

"Mr. Rowe was a sucker for a sad story," said Feidt. "One evening a dapper fellow came in and asked for the manager. He told Rowe his car broke down and he needed

$25 and that he'd come right back and pay him. We all knew it was a fake story, but Rowe insisted the man was honest and had me give him the money. He put a voucher in the cash box. The man never returned. It got to be a joke for several years and we'd tease him about that voucher. Finally, one year it disappeared."

In order to stretch the hotel's seasonal use for several years, tour groups came to Florida from New York for a summer weekend. Jean Renwick Ott did everything to keep them cool and comfortable. She checked the wind direction and opened the coolest rooms. If the breeze changed, she had to run down the hall, opening all rooms on the opposite side of the building. All in all, summer business was too hectic and too unprofitable to make it worthwhile. Management never tried to book conventions to extend the resort season, limiting themselves to the two prime winter month's business.

It was a close-knit family that staffed the Don. During the season, Rowe lived in the penthouse, but because of poor health, he moved to a two room suite, 101 and 102, on the first floor. He loved his people so much that he said he was going to will the hotel to them. This is how he instructed his attorney, Erle Askew, but the new will was never signed.

ENJOY THE BEAUTIES OF THE WINTER SEASON

On one of the most beautiful beaches in the world, furnished and serviced for sun and water bathing. Luncheons served on the beach when desired. Get a sun tan and glow of health that will make you feel proud as well as good. Go home rejuvenated, and feeling fit. The beach does these things to you.

Horseback parties arranged, golf close by, fishing parties in deep and shallow water, dancing, concerts, etc. American Plan. Rates Reasonable.

OPENING DATE: DECEMBER 15th

DON CE-SAR BEACH HOTEL

Thomas J. Rowe, Owner and Manager, Pass-a-Grille

12 Miles From St. Petersburg, Florida

Scene of Brilliant Fashion Show and Regatta

The annual West Coast Fashion Show at the palatial Don-Ce-Sar hotel will be one of the most outstanding events of the season. Styles with a zip and verve, an index to the latest dictates of world famous designers of apparel for men and women, will be shown. One hundred models will parade down the long runway in the center of the ball room.

The combination of setting, beautiful models, gorgeous clothes, the regatta, music and entertainment will make this event one of the greatest attractions of the west coast.

Further interest has been added to the program in secur-ing the services of a nationally known stylist of Paris and Boston, who will arrive in St. Petersburg the early part of February. She will be assisted by Miss Adel Sullivan of Philadelphia.

The show will be much larger and more spectacular as so many new features have been added. There will be seating capacity for three thousand. The Pass-a-Grille Yacht Club will stage the regatta in the afternoon.

Merchants from St. Petersburg, Tampa, Clearwater, Sarasota and Orlando will display merchandise.

Advertisement from the West Coast Informant 1937.

Chapter VI

END OF AN ERA

I n 1940, the hotel closed as usual for the season. Art Feidt drove north for the summer and the rest of the staff scattered, never knowing life at the Don Ce-Sar would never be the same.

It was a hot May afternoon. Thomas Rowe was looking over the deserted lobby, inventorying work that had to be done before the next season. With a sudden cry, he staggered then collapsed. His secretary Lucille Wilson came running. "He slowly came to," she says. "He struggled to his feet. Such a proud man, he wouldn't even let me take his arm to help him up the few steps to his rooms."

Dr. Post, the Don Ce-Sar physician, was called and Mary Berg took over with two other nurses to help her for an around-the-clock vigil.

"Mr. Rowe refused to leave the Don to go into town to the hospital so we had an oxygen tent and special emergency equipment installed in his suite," said Nurse Berg.

When his attorney, Erle Askew, rushed out with the new will, the nurses refused to witness Rowe's signature, saying he was "in no condition to make such a decision." After another attack, he lost consciousness. He died May 5, 1940.

His widow, Mary Rowe, bought a large monument for him and had him buried in St. Petersburg's Royal Palm Cemetery.

A three page obituary in the Gulf Beach News mourned the loss of this great man who had played a pioneer role in Florida's development. It said in part:

"Many famous local men were his friends; R.L. Hope, James Bourne, Judge T. Frank Hobson, E.P. Cody, Paul Poynter, Walter Fuller, Lew Brown, Erle Askew, Carlton Beard, Claude Strickland, Leo T. Sullivan,

Arthur Feidt were pall bearers for his funeral."

"He assisted Walter Fuller in securing the 'White Way' from Central Avenue to Boca Ciega Bay and secured the system of bridges and roads which linked the island with the mainland at that time."

"Rowe had become a veritable "father confessor" for business troubles. From the grocery store owner to the developer, he was the eyes through which they were able to see the future of the island. Pat Sergi, operator of the cottage colony at Lido Beach, said of his death, "I know of no greater calamity which could have befallen the beaches at this time."

Real estate associate Walter Fuller said of Rowe, "I have never known Mr. Rowe to go back on an agreement, or show discourtesy or lack of consideration. In times of stress and excitement, he never lost his perspective on long range principles and ideas. In every way, he was a wonderful friend, a wise advisor and a constructive citizen."

J. Harold Sommers said, "I have heard the Don Ce-Sar called 'Tom Rowe's crazy dream.' I call it 'Tom Rowe's monument.' The crazy dream has materialized. No one ever did more to encourage and inspire those who wished to create an attractive community along the Gulf shore. He pointed the way —— some day when he looks down from that great balcony above and sees his beloved Gulf Beaches lined with magnificent structures, he'll think, 'That's grand, boys, keep up the good work.' "

"The Don Ce-Sar is a monument to his memory, but by his kind personality, he built a monument in the hearts and minds of those who knew and loved him."

Some say the first time Mary Rowe came to the Don Ce-Sar was the day she took over as owner. For years, she and her husband had been separated. She was a well-educated woman, a true Virginian and a member of the University Women. She followed her husband to St. Petersburg but lived downtown even after he moved to the beach. He once filed for divorce, but dropped the case. According to Florida law at that time, he could not file again. Because of this impasse, she inherited Rowe's entire estate but not without a court fight.

Erle Askew and Rowe's housekeeper contested the settlement and were finally awarded $60,000.

When she took over the hotel, Mrs. Rowe hired Julian Hillman, a hotel manager from Atlantic City, for the coming season. The staff members didn't want to work for a new man, though. The fine "cultured" families who returned resented his "Miami Beach-like" management and stopped coming. Consequently the hotel was in financial trouble again.

In addition, not aware of business practices, Mrs. Rowe was having trouble with her attorney. He'd have her sign papers to release property and money but she never received the money nor had an accounting. At one point, he sold the hotel garages, which further crippled the hotel operations. Her banker then advised her to make attorney Frank Harris president of the corporation. Mrs. Rowe, surprisingly enough, heeded that advice.

When Harris took over, he bought new land across from the administration building to build new garages. In May 1941, Art Feidt was named manager, and the year ran smoothly.

Red velvet draperies were replaced by decorators from Willson-Chase, a St. Petersburg department store. "Mary Rowe was the most determined woman in the world," Feidt said. "She would go downtown, buy remnants and come back and try to cover wicker chair seats in the sun room herself. It was quite a hodge-podge when she finished.

"She obviously wanted us to remember her husband because she had his portrait hung in the lobby."

"With her companion, she stayed year-round in the hotel and kept close watch on everything," said Feidt.

December 7, 1941 the Japanese bombed Pearl Harbor. Within hours, telegrams poured in with cancellations for the coming season and within weeks 50 percent of the reservations were cancelled.

Less than 100 rooms were filled all winter. The gaiety was gone. Everyone was worried. Gas was rationed. Waiters, cooks, clerks and janitors were drafted. It was a long, lean winter, with rumors that enemy submarines were lurking offshore.

Jean Ott thought two men acted suspiciously. She intercepted a telegram, called the FBI, and the men were arrested on the way to the train. They were German spies transmitting code messages from New Jersey to Germany.

"Jack-of-all-trades" Bellman Sam Wynn no longer took guests to the roof to see the view, saying, "Fifteen hundred miles to the west of here is Corpus Christi, Texas." Instead, Civil Defense spotters like Yi Roberts Daily and her father scoured the skies for enemy ships and subs. (Yi still tells about the precarious climbs across a catwalk in the tower where you could look down an air shaft to the ground ten stories below).

Art Feidt said of that year, "We always had good credit. We got through the season –– and were the only hotel able to pay off its laundry bill ––but that was the end. When we closed, we had $1500 in the bank and little prospects for another season."

Frank Harris conferred with government representatives to find a wartime use for the Don. Even though he had an offer from the Army to buy the property, he was dickering with the Navy on a better deal. He favored their proposition to open the Don as a Naval officers' residence club for $1,000 per guest, and have the civilian staff run it. The hotel would realize about $100,000 profit and Mrs. Rowe would still own the building after the war.

Harris was in Washington finalizing the deal when the Army, hearing the Navy was interested, grabbed the hotel out from under them. With Florida Senator Claude Pepper's help, the Army had the property condemned and then bought it outright for its assessed value of $450,000. (It had cost Rowe $1,500,000). Mary Rowe had little left after paying $300,000 to the bond holders, $60,000 to Askew and his client, and taxes.

Feidt was called back from Toledo where he had gone to work for the summer. He and Harris returned to find the building locked and sentries posted outside. No provision had been made to feed the guards. The neighbors brought them food for three weeks while they were on duty.

The hotel staff came to work one morning to find they were locked out and, moreover, out of jobs.

A lieutenant and twenty men were sent to take inventory.

"You talk about gold-bricking," Feidt laughed. "It took them three months to inventory. The lieutenant made his men carry every stick of furniture and china into the ballroom. He walked around without his shirt, but he made his men wear full uniform. That summer it was 105 to 110 degrees inside."

"What a martinet!" He wouldn't even let us get into out files. They seized everything," Feidt said.

It was a final and dramatic end to the luxurious era of Thomas Rowe's Don Ce-Sar.

Chapter VII

THE GOLDEN AGE OF SERVICE

When the Army hurriedly purchased the luxury hotel, they hadn't analyzed the practicality of converting it into a hospital. As a result, the Don struck out twice in one year before finding its true role in World War II.

The first was a story of too much. It was an expensive undertaking. Two hundred thousand dollars was spent converting the building. Major John Schindler directed the remodelling. Offices, clinics and laboratories occupied the ground floor. Partitions were torn down between hotel rooms to create wards. Two operating rooms were constructed on the eighth floor, and the elegant ballroom became a War Department Theater that would accommodate 400 servicemen.

When it was ready in December 1942, the hospital was already inadequate to handle 800 sick calls a day for 16,000 troops stationed nearby. Mary Berg, now a Red Cross nurse, tended patients on cots that lined the halls. Six months after opening, there were 60,000 men to serve and the hospital could not handle the patient load.

The Don's next assignment as a sub base hospital for MacDill Air Force Base in Tampa fizzled out because there were too few patients. There was, to be sure, some interesting experimental treatment held there with a new drug called penicillin, but not enough use was made of the Don to warrant the government's investment which had now grown to $650,000.

In February, 1944, the Don Ce-Sar began its "golden age" as a new Air Force Convalescent Center affectionately referred to by its staff and patients as "The Don."

If brick, tile and mortar could talk, the Don Ce-Sar would reminisce about those years it served sheltering shattered airmen as they slowly found the road back to normalcy. In her many lives, the grand matron of the Gulf of Mexico was never more needed then as a haven of rest and rehabilitation.

The new center was the brainchild of General N.W. Grant. Concerned that battle-fatigued airmen were scattered in hospitals on six bases around the country, he conceived the plan of gathering them in one location for special psychiatric care. At that time they had mingled with new trainees who had not been overseas and were, in some cases, endangering the trainees morale. The Don was perfectly suited for its new role because of its fine recreational facilities, the solubrious climate of Florida's Gulf Coast and the ease with which hotel facilities could be converted to serve the patients.

Colonel R.E. Elvins, commanding officer, seized every opportunity to hasten the recovery of his 650 patients. After six to eight weeks, their cases were reviewed and they were either sent back overseas or to non-combatant duties or else returned to civilian life. He and his staff were dedicated men and women with a mission. Together they guided their patients "From the dusk of despair to the dawn of new ambitions."

Only men suffering from overseas combat fatigue were admitted to the Don. An interesting exception to this was the time two veterans of the Women's Army Corps were sent there after the London robot bomb blitz in 1944. It must have been an unusual experience for these girls who were "surprised and delighted with the treatment and consideration" they received as Don Ce-Sar patients.

Most patients looked healthy and suntanned. Their emotional problems were hard to detect, however. Perhaps it was the ideal climate and the beauty of their surroundings that hastened their recovery. During the day, every floor echoed to the sound of laughter, singing, shouting, and animated conversation. There was always an atmosphere of universal good humor.

These men understood they were not "temporarily

insane." They looked on themselves as nervous or emotional casualties rather than mental cases. They talked freely about combat experiences. When watching war films in the theater, they criticised technical details of battle and yelled their derision at any "unconvincing flag-waving." Most enlisted men were ready to be discharged because they felt they had "done their share" or they were afraid of another tour of combat duty. The officers were usually less direct in their comments.

There was a good relationship between the airmen and the residents of the nearby town of Pass-a-Grille. "Actually, it was such a good relationship that the chaplain performed an average of two weddings a week!" Red Cross director Margaret Cavanaugh said. Mabel Hastings and Dr. John Daly, an Air Force rehabilitation instructor, were the first couple to be married in the chapel. (They celebrated their anniversary in the newly-renovated hotel in December 1973).

Residents caught in the tensions of a war and the doldrums of a resort community without tourists opened their arms to the men and their families.

If the patients from the center were rambunctious on Saturday nights in town, the Military Police soon straightened them out and took them back to the Don. Dr. Viola Lancaster can tell many tales of patients who crawled up fire escapes when they were out after curfew. One Sunday morning, she heard one young serviceman calling out for help in the Blind Pass current, and she jumped in and saved his life.

There was always a battle with the Pinellas County Water System. Residents and military personnel fought together to secure enough water and adequate pressure.

Sometimes water pressure was so low that open faucets on even the first and second floors of the Don drew no water. When a prominent Pass-a-Grille citizen was caught covered with soap in the shower when the pressure failed, action was taken immediately to boost the pressure.

Photography was one of the interest groups organized for patients.

Edgar Kennedy stopped off to entertain at the Don on his USO tour.

Bomb-a-Dears, girls from St. Petersburg, helped in "resocialization" process.

Patient's mess hall in 1943 as it was on the fifth floor complete with velvet draperies and Spanish tile floor (now the location of the opulent King Charles II Dining Room).

Margaret Cavanaugh organized the Red Cross activities at the Don.

During the hurricane of October 1944, residents were sheltered at the Don, thereby temporarily increasing its occupancy to 3,000. With power lines down, they lost contact with the outside world and an emergency transmitter had to be operated on the fifth floor while the storm raged.

By morning, the Don Ce-Sar looked like a country fair as children raced through the lobby followed by dogs and cats. The only evidence of the storm's fury was the broken flagpole outside and a little rain water on the lower floor.

Those were the days when the Don was filled and things were happening.

Colonel Elvins was pleased with the progress his patients made at The Don. His high record for rehabilitations brought visitors from other sections of the

Water sports were part of the recreation play at the Air Force Convalescent Center.

military and from foreign countries as well to study the pilot program begun there.

Reader's Digest and *Mademoiselle Magazine* did special features on the program applauding the staff for "conserving human lives." Several other centers were organized following the same pattern.

Col. Elvins was compelled to battle Washington for more usable space and for appropriations for repairs. He hoped to buy the nearby Towers (later destroyed by fire) and Rellim Hotels to expand the center's capacity to more than 1,000. A new Red Cross building was under construction in April 1945, and it looked like there would be continued expansion. On all sides the Don experiment seemed successful.

Imagine Elvins' and his staff's dismay in the midst of all this good news, when they received a confidential

Colonel Elvins (second from left) welcomes movie star Cary Grant, February 1945.

letter from Washington in June 1945 ordering the center closed and the transfer of all personnel and patients.

Without warning, without recourse, by sudden political action, the successful Air Force Convalescent Center was phased out by September 1945.

Once more the Don Ce-Sar building had struck out. Col. Elvins finished his journal with this heart-breaking comment: "The Don was dead, a noble experiment was dead —— dead at the hand of an administrative order."

"Don Roger" masthead of the A.A.F. newspaper.

Chapter VIII

OFFICE WITH A MILLION DOLLAR VIEW

Patients were soon transferred to other hospitals. When doctors and nurses arrived in June for training, they had a surprise waiting for them. The Don closed so rapidly that their orders had no time to keep up with the change.

Down the street, wrecking crews were dismantling the still uncompleted Red Cross Building.

Some of the barracks "hutments" would be combined and sold as beach houses to townspeople.

By September 1945, all was still and vacant, but a great change would take place before December.

Returning veterans with their applications for G.I. benefits and various problems created a need for a large Veteran's Administration Regional Office in the St. Petersburg area and the Don was the logical candidate for the new job.

The new tenants removed more partitions, creating large offices from several hotel rooms to house the hundreds of government employees manning the VA installation. By March 1945 all the work of the downtown St. Petersburg office and the Bay Pines office was consolidated at the Don. Veterans from every county of Florida were served by the new Regional Office.

Director H.F. Dickensheets moved into the luxurious penthouse apartment. Thomas Rowe's greeting over the entrance was hurriedly removed by Dickensheet's orders. Critics who read the inscription, "Come all ye who seek rest and health for here it is abundant," would say, "Aha, I always knew that all a VA worker did was rest and play. This proves it."

The inspirational scene for "Moon Over Don Ce-Sar."

Gradually the once-luxurious hotel's interiors were stripped to the bare walls and painted "government green."

Down came the marquee. Rooms full of furniture, draperies, Oriental rugs and bronze fixtures were loaded into government trucks and carried away. Many things turned up in downtown hotels.

The lobby fountain was destroyed and sealed off.

Many workers shared the sentiments of Betty Beggs who wrote this letter and sealed it in the fountain before it was covered by flooring. The note lay undiscovered for 25 years. The shredded remnants read:

"The Passing of the Fish Pool, July 28, 1948. At this spot in the center of the spacious Don Ce-Sar stood a fish pool covered with imported tile. The manager, Mr. H.F. Dickensheets, decided that the fish pool was unsightly and in the way of pedestrian traffic, so it must be destroyed. During the heyday of this hotel, this fish pool was a spot of beauty sitting in the center of this spacious lobby. It is with much regret that Mr. S.F. Kuban, head carpenter, upon instructions of Mr. W.D. Goodale, superintendent of the building, demolished this pool. If this letter should be found, it is hoped that it can be published in the newspaper. (signed) T.L. Hazen, G.R. Lee and Miss Betty Beggs."

In November 1973, it was published in the St. Petersburg Times by columnist Dick Bothwell.

The Don's ballroom now housed endless rows of steel filing cabinets of veteran's records. The entire building had become a businesslike shell housing office equipment where workers looked up from their desk to daydream occasionally as they gazed out over the sparkling water of the Gulf of Mexico.

Dickensheets was the only one fortunate enough to call the Don his home and his livingroom had an unparalleled view from the ninth floor penthouse.

It was awkward receiving guests though and Mrs. Dickensheets was often lonely in her tower home. When she knew guests were coming, she'd meet them at

43

the front door on the ground floor and conduct them through the deserted lobby to the elevator and then up to the penthouse. It must have been eerie living with the many ghosts of the Don's past as the wind whistled down corridors and around the building.

From Washington came rumblings that a Senate investigation was questioning the economy of 100 office workers occupying 300 rooms and 300 baths in a 10-story building. After the committee's visit, the Dickensheets quietly moved to a house in the nearby community.

In 1952, several other agencies, State Services and U.S. Fish and Wildlife moved into the Don Ce-Sar to join the Veteran's Administration. General Services Administration then became custodian of the Don as it was now government real estate, not just the VA's.

During the next 23 years, thousands of ex GIs visited the Don for medical treatment or to apply for government benefits.

Men like Syd Teskey, veteran of three wars, went to the Out Patient Clinic for diagnostic tests. When they told Syd he might soon be blind without a cataract operation, he was eager to go to the VA Hospital at Bay Pines for surgery. He prayed for his sight. When the bandages were removed he was overjoyed to see again, and wrote his happy song, "Moon Over Don Ce-Sar," because he connected the place with his recovery.

Others like Dr. Halburt Earp remember the many years they worked at the Don. He supervised the medical services from his office in the north wing.

In 1955, Fred Lumley was among many civilian volunteers who watched for planes from the penthouse as part of the civil defense program.

For the sleepy town of Don Ce-Sar and nearby Pass-a-Grille the presence of a $2,500,000 smokeless industry was a shock. Traffic on the two-lane road to the mainland was so bad that local residents carefully avoided driving at 4:30 pm when workers poured out of the Don for their homeward trek.

44

Of course, many workers stimulated the growth of the nearby beach municipalities by renting or buying homes near the Don. (These many small incorporated towns were later consolidated to form the City of St. Petersburg Beach).

Some offices were eventually air-conditioned, but most were hot and humid yet never without a salty breeze from the Gulf. Lunch hours found some workers picnicking on the fire escapes or on the beach, taking healthful walks or else gazing out to sea. The Don was more than just a place to work. Those who worked there developed an affection for their deserted hotel-office building with a million dollar view.

As building superintendent, Alex Saverino was to maintain the building according to minimum standards. This was especially frustrating because the government always seemed to budget too little for repairs. Age and the many years of abuse were beginning to take their toll.

His other headache was satisfying the neighboring residents who seemed to keep a direct line open to Washington. Many complained "the public is using our beach" and he patiently relayed all the calls to GSA in Atlanta.

One neighbor with "Washington connections" called almost daily complaining that the grass needed cutting or the flag wasn't flying. Saverino had to put up the flag even when it meant climbing the pole or holding it out the window himself.

Many continued to write a Congressman about the "building's dilapidated appearance."

In 1961, drastic measures had to be taken to keep the rain out. It cost the government $235,000 for waterproofing, replacing wood around windows, repairing the red tile roof, new wiring, a modern generator and a complete coat of pink paint.

After that, no further maintenance was ever authorized. It was estimated that updating the Don would cost about $3,000,000. The appraisers erroneously assumed the building was a "flimsy" stucco over lath combination that wasn't fireproof. They recommended that all walls should be torn out and replaced with cement blocks. The cost of central air conditioning would be prohibitive, they claimed.

"Since it is no longer economically feasible for the government to utilize the building," they reported, "we favor building a new Federal building and vacating the Don Ce-Sar."

"It broke my heart to watch that beautiful building run-down," said Saverino.

Local residents were thrown into a quandry at the prospect of what would happen to the discarded Don.

Colonel Frank T. Hurley had approached the GSA several years before with letters from hotel men who offered a million dollars for it, but at that time the government had turned it down. Then Col. Hurley suggested that it should be converted into a hospital to serve the beaches and nearby South Pasadena on the mainland.

Dr. George L. Greene of the Pass-a-Grille Church headed a committee of businessmen consisting of Bush Locknane, Robert Lamb, Donald Colville, Charles Drew, Richard Ayers and Ted Lundberg who studied possible uses for the property. They sought an "acceptable" government agency or a private developer. Some tried in vain to attract a research bureau of marine biology, hoping to combat misuse of the property or its abandonment. What to do with the Don Ce-Sar became a major local problem that might affect all residents.

Time dragged on. The new building in St. Petersburg wasn't ready as soon as predicted. St. Petersburg Beach mayors changed, members of the committee died or moved away. When Mayor Bill Coletti inherited the problem, he organized a new committee that included Frank T. Hurley, Jr., then a city commissioner. Still nothing definite turned up as a solution to the problem.

On November 27, 1967 the VA began moving out and by Spring of 1969, the last remnants of the Out Patient's Clinic moved out. The lonely abandoned building

Crumbling architectural boxes -- evidence "the destroyers" used to build their case to have the Don demolished.

became the blackboard for protest slogans and a target for vandals. Residents called the police when they saw a teen-age boy hanging out a window atop the Don. Drifters moved in. Pigeons flew in broken windows and a white owl resided in the south tower. What once had been a beauty spot now became a community blemish.

Dear Reader,

Historians are third person people. They write history and seldom make it. Moreover, they usually write history objectively as seen from a vantage point years after an event occurred. When I began writing about the Don's past (in 1971), I became an active part of its present and future. I am proud that I was able to help in the campaign that saved the Don Ce-Sar from the wrecking ball. Since I find it impossible to write the next few chapters without saying "I did this" or "I thought that," I hope you will bear with me while I shift from third to first person for the rest of the story.

June Hurley Young

Chapter IX

A CLOSE CALL

General Services Administration was trying to dispose of the Don Ce-Sar, the neighbors were frantic to have something done. Many were predicting that the building would become a gutted ruin, haven for unsavory drifters, not only an eyesore but a potential danger to residents. Bits of the trim had fallen or cracked and many felt it dangerous to even walk around the Don.

It was at the point that "many were saying the only thing to do is tear it down" that I became involved in events that led to saving the Don.

Like most residents, I admired the pink castle. Beautiful things are an inspiration to many people. The more I found out about the history of the Don, the more fascinated I became to learn more and to publicize the building's value. I wanted to save it from being demolished and find a way that once again people could enjoy the healthful, wholesome life that its facilities could provide.

Alex Saverino said, "From the penthouse, on a clear day, you can see forever." My inspiration was that view I wanted many to share.

Saverino was my foot in the door. For over a year I had asked the Mayor if I might see the inside of the Don, but the opportunity never came. The word was that it was decided that the building was about to be demolished to make room for a public park. I was thinking I'd need a Congressional order to get in, when, on a hunch, I called the Federal Building and asked who was in charge of the Don. That's when I met Alex Saverino, January 14, 1971. He was the one who answered the phone and quickly responded, "Why do you want to go in?"

The words were out before I had time to think, "I'm writing a newspaper article and I need more information."

"Oh, there's a man out there who's writing a book, General Rives. He has a whole set of pictures and information that could help you. When do you want to see the building?"

"I can meet you there in a hour," I said, and Alex said that would be fine.

Sarah and Russell Hughes, the neighbors to the south and two contractors, Dick Williams and Jeff Stone, went along for the tour. I wanted an opinion on the feasibility of tackling such a big renovation job from someone with know-how.

The interior was magnificent, even with the broken glass and remnants of the papers left by the government workers as they hurried away. Every room was flooded with sunlight from the high arched windows, and from every room there was a view of sparkling surf and white sand.

Saverino apologized for the building's poor condition, but I saw only its sunlighted spaciousness. What a waste— a ballroom with 6,000 square feet of space vacant while St. Petersburg cried for convention facilities. He explained that the high upkeep and the cost of air-conditioning sparked the government's decision to phase out the Don and build a 5 million dollar office downtown.

We analyzed the new power plant and wiring. My experts pointed out that plumbing would be a big item in the renovation. Undoubtedly, it would all have to be removed.

Saverino suggested that the walls around the windows might have to be taken out.

I was anxious to begin writing. My friend, Charles Schmutz, another neighbor, was needling me to do something about the Don.

Armed with some old clippings and my notes, I began. I was in a hurry, because I sensed time was running out for the Don. The local papers weren't interested, but I had a tentative go ahead from Mal Gibson, editor of *Accent Magazine* of the *Tampa Tribune.*

Saverino had some historical photos of the construction of the Don that he said I could borrow, and I wanted him to check the facts of my story so I met him at his office.

While I was waiting for him to come back from lunch, I looked around at the photos on the wall. There was an organization picture of GSA and Leonard Sheppard was the name under the man at the top. I jotted down his name and the address of GSA in Atlanta in case I might need it.

When Saverino arrived, he was pleased with the story and encouraged me to go on with it. I was fascinated by the old photos. We were examining the one that showed the completed building without stucco and ornamentation. "Look, in the blowup you can see the blocks around the windows. It's not stucco over lath," I exclaimed. This further affirmed the value of the Don as it was, a solid fortress under the frills.

While I was busy writing, things were happening in

The historic photo that proved all exterior walls were made of hollow tile.

the community. The Woman's Club was told the Don was to be demolished. Don Ce-Sar residents met to discuss action to take. They didn't want a public park, but they suggested the empty site could be divided into lots for several single-family residents. Wrecking companies were making bids on the job. Some said the rubble would make a fine jetty to nourish the North beach.

In Clearwater, William Dockerty announced to the County Commission that he could get the Republican delegation to help Pinellas County acquire the Don Ce-Sar property as a public park.

No longer able to wait, I called Leonard Sheppard of GSA long distance in Atlanta. He seemed surprised to hear what was happening in St. Petersburg Beach. It was his opinion that the people wanted the site for a park. As head of the division of property management and disposal, he was eager to hear what was really going on and called me back that same afternoon to continue our conversation. He explained all the channels and red tape concerned in obtaining the Don.

My *Accent* article "Pink Elephant or Sleeping Beauty," February 14, 1971, was the first note of hope suggesting there was a future for the old hotel. The tide was turned. Citizens responded and Mayor Dick Misener called a special town meeting. After the discussion that night, he said, "Mrs. Hurley, do you intend to do this by yourself or do you want the city's help?" He named a committee to work with the city to try to save the Don.

My article attracted people with information about the past; Art Feidt, a former manager; Leon and Jean Ott, Lucille Wilson of the hotel staff; and Carlton Beard, Rowe's contractor.

One Saturday we gathered outside the Don waiting to take a tour. It was the "Save the Don Committee's" first opportunity to go inside. Paul Resop, Joanne Merritt, Junerose Wissker, Percy Meeker, Ray Martin, Carol Curotto Upham, Bush Locknane, Bill Ruscoe, Virginia Harris, Ed Stanton, John Fairfield and I were there. Art Johnson of WLCY TV news was making a movie for the half hour show we would produce. We all waited and the guard refused to let us in. His angry German Shepherd lunged at us from the door. The Don was "off limits" to visitors; GSA didn't like the furor all the unfavorable publicity had caused.

Even our local police were asking us to leave. It took a special order from Congressman Bill Young to get the committee admitted for an inspection. Later, Senator Lawton Chiles also helped us with our drive. The pressure was on. We had one month until April

15 to come up with an acceptable plan or another agency might get the property or have it torn down.

We all worked estimating costs and contacting businessmen like August Busch, Jack Eckerd, and Jim Walters. Their letters were courteous but disinterested. Floyd Christian, Superintendent of the State Department of Education, was encouraging us to proceed with the project. He would study the possibility of the State's use and let us know what he heard.

It was the government bulletin that read, "A city can purchase property at fair market value and determine its use," that gave us our case. This was our proposal to GSA. We said we wanted to buy the building and see that a developer who would renovate it would help us. Our City Manager sent in another request to get the property free to use as a park and Florida Presbyterian College (now Eckerd College) put in a request. Eckerd withdrew, but GSA was confused by two contradictory requests from St. Petersburg Beach. When the dust cleared, our request to buy the building was the only remaining offer.

Sheppard and his attorney came to discuss price. We had one developer who wouldn't name a figure and another who would go to $300,000 to convert the Don to a nursing home. We were stymied to find out GSA thought a fair price was three times what we could get anyone to offer.

There was no avenue we didn't pursue, no source of development we didn't explore. Over and over I climbed those eighteen flights of stairs to the penthouse with prospective buyers. I wrote articles and the committee met weekly for long discussions. Ray Martin carried continuous articles in his *Pinellas Review* for local businessmen.

Bill Ruscoe and I spent a day with Frank Harris, former Don Ce-Sar president, in Sarasota where we asked James Haley for information about how Congress would act on a proposal when we got one.

It was July 1971 when some of my articles and a radio

interview caught the attention of William Bowman, Jr., owner of the Holiday Inn in St. Petersburg Beach. A St. Louis man, he pioneered the franchise movement and had been active in thirteen Holiday Inns. He was looking for "a new kind of challenge," a unique hotel that wouldn't fit the stereotyped mold he was used to.

He and his attorney Adrian Bacon examined the Don. Bowman liked it immediately. I had just assured him the roof was relatively new when he stepped into a hole of soft tar. To Adrian's dismay, Bill said abruptly, "I want a 90-day option at $400,000. "Wait a minute, I can't do that," I answered. I told him there would be meetings, letters to GSA and he'd have to show his plans along with an acceptable offer to the committee.

The long summer was endless with meetings. Another local developer was interested but wouldn't commit himself to a price until he made expensive surveys. The committee was divided so we agreed to submit both proposals and let the City Commission make the decision. They favored Bowman's plan as being more concrete.

It was March 1972 when Leonard Sheppard turned over the keys to Mayor Dick Misener, who transferred them to William Bowman, Jr.

What a celebration the committee, the Commission, and all the lending agencies and workers had that night. Bill Bowman, his wife Anne and sons Bill III and John Mallory came from St. Louis for the banquet. It had taken one year and two months to accomplish what many had said was impossible.

The forty-four year old Don Ce-Sar built by Thomas Rowe would have a second chance to become the West Coast's most opulent resort.

Chapter X

A RETURN TO ELEGANCE

From the first, Bill Bowman viewed the Don Ce-Sar as a "sleeping beauty." Bringing the hotel back to life was just the kind of challenge he was looking for. As the new owner, he changed the spelling of the hotel's name to Don CeSar, omitting the hyphen.

Outside the public saw the broken windows and peeling paint. From the Bayway Bridge, the Don's beautiful profile cancelled out the signs of age.

It took a man who could visualize, a man who saw beyond the vacant lobby littered with broken glass and the penthouse full of pigeons. The corridors were bare and dreary, floored with broken asphalt tile and her ceilings sprouted row after row of fluorescent lights left by the last tenants.

His first good fortune was Bob Vodicka's answer to an ad he ran in the *Wall Street Journal*. Retired from the service, Bob was available as an architectural consultant. The two men were well-paired in creativity and drive. They were in as complete accord as brothers and caught up in the exhaltation of bringing elegance to the long neglected hotel.

In his plush downtown office, Bowman covered the walls with giant photographs of the Don. His inspiration was a full-color architect's drawing of the finished hotel, an ornate complex with an overpass over Gulf Boulevard, its grounds filled with pools, fountains, a putting green, and tennis courts.

Residents eagerly watched the Don for signs of new life. The crews put up a tall chain-link fence to keep out the curious. This, plus the building's state of dishevelment, gave it the look of an abandoned prison camp.

A rag-taggle group of drifters filed in at 8 and out at 4. Anyone who wanted a few days work at minimum wage had the job as long as he wanted to work. It was C.L. Pyatt and Don Dye who spent their time keeping the pot smokers from kidnapping the elevator. It was a hard job routing the sluggish workers who found it easy to lose themselves in the maze of deserted rooms and hallways. When they ran out of strong young men, they hired girls for the less heavy work.

It was exhausting work, ripping out old doors and partitions and shoveling out the tons of debris. The tearing down took until January 1973. Heavy porcelain bathroom fixtures were piled in the parking lot alongside the rows of lighting fixtures and warped and peeling green doors. The litter added to the Don's dishevelment.

Bowman abandoned his plan to put aluminum windows everywhere. Pane by pane, 13,000 pieces of glass were removed, the wood was scraped, repaired, replaced and repainted. Of all the jobs, this was the most tedious and time-consuming, but he preserved the hotel's most lovely natural asset – the original windows.

It was no easy job erasing four decades of neglect from the face of the Don CeSar.

Modern fiberglass molded bathroom units were trucked across the Skyway and the Bayway, hoisted by cranes and swung in through large openings in the walls, and snapped into place. When the crane slipped, one of the modular bathrooms crashed into the chain-fence.

Wiring and plumbing was all replaced and the new air conditioning ducts were hidden in the walls.

In the 1930's someone carried a meat chopping block full of termites to the fifth floor kitchen. That family became the Don's oldest and most prolific. It cost Bowman $40,000 to evict them. No one could put an exterminating tent over the ten-story building. Instead, every window had to be sealed, the interior saturated with tons of poison, and left for several weeks. That siege plus a series of smoke bombs routed the pigeons from the penthouse. Still every day a workman would find some of the birds flying in the corridors. The

William Bowman, Jr. discusses his plans with Carlton Beard, the Don Ce-Sar's contractor who built it for Thomas J. Rowe.

last bedraggled straggler was still flying around on the fifth floor the day the Don opened.

The first part to be finished was the first floor of the North wing which would house the office of Bowman Development Company.

It took heavy-duty drills to break through the concrete slab flooring to make a new entrance-way. For the first time, Vodicka could see the building's construction. "It had double the tensile strength we had imagined. Concrete cures for ninety years. This was diamond-hard and only half that old. The floor was two feet thick concrete mixed with gravel and reinforced with heavy twisted iron cable. Rowe and his contractor believed in 'overbuilding.' "You'd never find this construction today," said Vodicka. In over forty years it showed little effect of settling and no major cracks. "What a crime it would have been to demolish it."

The finished office was paneled in walnut and cork. The floors were covered with expensive terra cotta tile or thick carpeting, and the foyer was covered with smoked mirror. Every detail to the heavy carved doors, antique hardware, draperies and brass chandeliers was luxurious.

Such a comfortable office was a reminder of the level of elegance that would be achieved in the rest of the building which now looked so ravaged.

Bowman moved his office into the Don CeSar in February 1973, the same month that he moved his family to Florida. No more would they regard themselves as residents of St. Louis.

With the valuable furnishings and office equipment in the Don, it was important someone be on the premises night and day. Recently someone had started a fire on the ninth floor and vandalism was always a problem.

C.L. Pyatt and Bill Bowman shared the duty and stayed in the office overnight.

Late one night Bowman heard a noise, grabbed his rifle and shouted, "Who's there?" He flung open the door. In the shadows a man in pajamas was pointing a rifle at him. He almost blasted a hole in the new mirrored wall before he realized what he saw was his own reflection.

Everyone was curious to know what was happening inside the Don. The newsmen wanted stories. The mail was filled with notes from well-wishers and requests for rooms and dates for banquets and conventions.

With a worried expression, Bowman would shake his head, "Just let me get this place open and then I'll worry about who'll use it. I can't commit myself on an opening day yet." It seemed the whole community was holding its breath, counting the days to see the finished Don CeSar.

Bowman and his interior designer, Lou Chiodini, traveled to all parts of the country buying ironwork, fixtures, paintings, tile, and furniture. "I'd be bogged down on some job in St. Louis and Bill would fly into town. All he had to say was, 'Come on Lou, let's go,' and I'd be ready. It was the most exciting job finding the right things for the hotel," recalls Chiodini.

One of the biggest challenges was finding the right window treatment for the large fan-shaped windows. Jesse Zimmerman of Cory's Fabrics remembers putting up and taking down the drapery on one of the ballroom windows ten times before everyone agreed it was the best design. The padded rust velvet cornice matches the shape of the window. The sheer fabric is shirred to a center and finished with a velvet rosette.

Zimmerman suggested a sequined valance for the dias in the ballroom, but Bowman preferred something more restrained. He had a rust velvet valance hung with medieval brass chains.

A specialist in space utilization, Bowman elevated an area to give his guests a better view. In the space under the floor he can hide wiring and duct work. In this way, he created the sunken grand ballroom, the intimate Buena Vista Bar and the many levels of the King Charles II diningroom on the fifth floor.

Originally the Don CeSar had a staircase from the ground floor to the lobby. With pillars like sturdy trees, the lobby rambled off spaciously toward the Gulf and toward the ballroom.

Like other successful hotel men, Bowman knew the importance of putting every space to work. When his crew discovered the abandoned fountain, he had them rebuild it as the focal point of a Spanish village surround-

Only a narrow passageway remains of the original lobby. Terra cotta tile, rugs, furniture and brass lamps add opulance.

Raised floors hide air-conditioning ducts and wiring and provide several levels in the newly-designed ballroom. The dance floor is all that remains of the original flooring. Austrian crystal chandeliers complete the ornate decor.

ed by shops. The original hardwood floor was covered with heavy Cuban tile.

The other part of the lobby was divided by partitions and openwork panels to make the Bar De Bazan and two intimate lounges, rest rooms and the Alcade Coffee Shop. The fine wood is beautifully varnished and polished in the coffee shop.

The Don's hotel rooms have rough stuccoed white walls, arches, beamed ceilings that give them a Spanish mission look.

Forty-five suites were made of combined rooms with kitchenettes. The handmade cabinets, like the fine furniture, were built by Dave Carpenter, the Don's own master craftsman. Each suite has sliding glass doors and an oval balcony with an iron railing, perhaps these were the most elegant touches added to the already ornate building.

Someone called the Don, "A Disneyesque Wedding Cake." All of the architectural frosting, the ropes, swags, urns and twisted pillars had to be copied. Carefully each was removed and a new cast made. Bowman was determined that everything would be replaced as it originally decorated the building. When fixing the roof, he had identical red Spanish tile made to replace those that were broken. It was a tedious job, removing and replacing all of them.

It would take 12,000 gallons of pink paint to cover the Don, but first all the cracks must be patched and the walls waterproofed. The workmen covered the finished windows with old curtains and bedspreads when they sprayed the walls "rouge," the same flamingo pink Rowe had chosen. When the first wing was completed, the sidewalk superintendents said the paint was too bright.

There was a legal tangle with the State for permission to build the 152-foot vehicular overpass over Gulf Boulevard. St. Petersburg Beach and Bowman's attorney, Adrian Bacon got the permission. One tie-up after another held up the construction company who contracted to do the work. In excavating, they hit sulphur springs

Balconies were added. Here is the original ground floor entrance before construction of the overpass.

and underground conduits. They were so far behind that it was beginning to look like opening day would find the hotel ready but the entranceway impassable.

In the time Bowman had been rebuilding, inflation had a strong grip on the economy. Labor, materials and

Overpass spans Gulf Boulevard, October 1973.

interest rates climbed to dizzying heights. His original plan to wait later to open was accelerated to combat rising costs. Staff began arriving from his hotels in Louisville, Kentucky, and Steamboat Springs, Colorado. Food and beverage departments were organizing, planning menus and food costs. They began accepting the reservations for banquets and conventions that came in the mail unsolicited. It seemed that in 1974 every event in town would be happening at the Don CeSar.

November 15th was the date set for the opening. With less than a month to go, the painters were only half finished with the exterior. The overpass had not yet spanned the road. Crews were working around the clock, seven days a week to finish the lobby, entrance way, the grand staircase, and the Spanish tiled registration desk. A nail-biting urgency hung over everyone. The opening was postponed to November 20th and finally set for Saturday, November 24th at 5 pm.

Chapter XI

A NEW BEGINNING

Saturday, November 24, 1973, is an unforgetable memory for those who waited eagerly for the twice postponed opening of the Don CeSar Resort Hotel.

City holdups on permits, work delays on the overpass and ramp, late furniture deliveries were only a few of the obstacles Bowman encountered. The country was feeling the pinch of a fuel shortage and the bottled gas companies refused new customers as they began rationing their supplies. Bowman had to find a new source of gas to run his gas-operated heating, cooling and kitchen appliances. A week before opening he had the crushing news that his closest friend, a man who had encouraged him in the first stages of the Don, Dr. Martin Hart, had died in St. Louis. Bowman left all of his "loose ends" to attend his friend's funeral and to comfort his family.

His team of workers placed furniture in rooms, waxed floors, worked around the clock, even through Thanksgiving Day (the Don's new chef fixed their holiday meal), and right up to 11 am Saturday —— the time of the ribbon cutting. Minutes before the ceremony John Roberts was still painting the giant scissors and fanning them to dry in time.

Mayor Dick Misener, Bill Bowman, and I drove the first car, a 1928 Plymouth, up the ramp. A mob of well-wishers greeted the car. Along with beach neighbors were those who figured in the Don CeSar's past; Carlton Beard, her builder; Jean Ott and Lucille Wilson, Thomas

*Mayor Dick Misener, owner William Bowman, Jr. and June
Hurley cut the ribbon at the opening ceremony, November
24, 1973. First sight-seers pour into the lobby opening
day.*

Rowe's office workers; Warren Hunnicut, Sr., Rowe's good friend; Alex Saverino, superintendent for the building for the Veteran's Administration.

With the ribbon cutting, the crowd swarmed down the carpeted stairs, exclaiming in awe over the glowing chandeliers and the golden richness of the new Don's interiors. Ahead lay the corridor of awninged shops and the Spanish tiled fountain. To the right lay another arcade of terra cotta tile with carpet islands and a quartette of velour lounge chairs. The revelers spilled down the halls, eager to see everything. The ballroom with its rust velvet draperies was arranged for the first banquet honoring the key people in the crusade to bring the Don back to life.

A trio played for dancing, a fandango dancer clicked her castinets in the tradition of the '30's and 50 guests enjoyed the cuisine of the new Don CeSar Resort Hotel.

The crowd cheered the announcement that veteran hotel man Phil Dross had accepted the managership of the Don CeSar. Dross, well-known for the years he managed the Tides Hotel and Bath Club, had in recent years brought new life to the Princess Martha Hotel. He would wind up his work there and assume the position at the Don the first of the year.

Mayor Dick Misener introduced special guests and Adrian Bacon, Bowman's attorney, gave appreciation toasts to Robert Vodicka, C.L. Pyatt, Don Dye and others of the Bowman team. It was the key man, Bill Bowman, who speechlessly remained in the background.

At 5 pm the Don welcomed the public. First nighters began arriving. Steve Vehmeier was checking the rooms over. Of the hundred ready, some were closed off with air-conditioning problems. Few of the televisions were working, but who would want to watch television on a night such as this?

Many local residents, like the Hubbards and the Lucases (descendants of Warren Webster), hired suites for the first night parties. Dinner reservations were closed at 400 but before the evening was over they served 600 guests. The halls swarmed with beauty, wealth and splendor. On the upper floor, one party spilled out into the hall and into another party. The dance floor was filled all evening. Strolling troubadours entertained in the lounge and at the dining room tables and later played for dancing.

One couple explored the second floor hall, looking for the room the husband used as an office during the time that the VA occupied the building. "I used to sit out on the fire escape and enjoy the view of the Gulf while I ate my bag-lunch," he reminisced.

One newspaper account said, "The Don almost didn't make her date with the public, Saturday. The grand opening found paint still drying on the walls, and many things still to be worked out, but her friends had come to see her, and they were ready to forgive anything for the experience."

Strangers wandered in and out of the parties, everyone was welcome. "Hi, I'm from Montreal. We stayed here back in 1938," exclaimed William Warmington who remembered staying in the Don's penthouse when the price was significantly less than the projected $250 per day to be charged now.

By 8 pm it looked like everyone had come for an all-night party. As diners are reluctant to leave, reservations backed up. Nobody minded waiting because the whole first floor was turned into one huge party.

By 10 pm first night guests settled into their rooms. Bellhops went to the local convenience store to buy more ice. The air conditioning was working again. No one seemed to miss it when the fresh Gulf breezes ruffled the draperies earlier.

On the second floor, a couple with a large German Shepherd wandered in looking for a party. The ballroom dinner was over at midnight but many were still dancing. Through the night, one or two lost souls wandered through the halls knocking on doors looking for the party they missed.

Sunday morning, the breeze blew cooly through the

Don's wide windows and the sun rose. A few overnight guests picked their way gingerly through the construction of the pool, tennis courts, and putting greens. Beach walkers and joggers paused to gaze at the pink splendor of the building, turned around and finished their trek.

Inside everything ran smoothly. The repair work was done, the remnants of the revelers swept up and the floor and furniture polished. The big news was "There's a new landmark in town. The Don CeSar Resort Hotel is open for business." Thomas Rowe built it and Bill Bowman brought it back to life.

New Landmark in Town

REFLECTION...............................2007

It has been thirty-three years and 22,000 copies of my book since I began the story of Don CeSar. In 1975, William Bowman Jr. was honored when his Don CeSar Resort Hotel became the first landmark on Florida's West Coast to be admitted to the Registry of Historic American Buildings. He bought the historic marker that explained the designation and the story of how the hotel survived the threat of demolition. The October night he celebrated the completion of the renovation by wining and dining 100 special guests in the ballroom.

Then, because of adverse market conditions, a gas shortage, domestic problems and a struggling resort year of 1974, owing only $6 million, he gave up ownership of the Don . On his fiftieth birthday, Oct. 24, 1975, he handed the keys over to his lender Connecticut General Insurance Co. They accepted the perfectly completed, furnished hotel but refused to take on the indebtedness for the furnishings and equipment. It took Bowman seven years more to complete the payments on that $700,000 bank loan for all the accoutrements he no longer owned. He walked away and never looked back. He lost his dream, his entire $2 million personal fortune and three years of hard work with nothing to show for it.

His loyal staff toasted him for his birthday in the St. Petersburg Beach Hilton Hotel, the showplace he built while renovating the Don.

In his office there he brainstormed the new motel concept he was formulating. A veteran of the early Holiday Inn franchises, he launched a new career of designing and building three new motels, La Casa, La Quinta and La Casa Grande. In his career he completed over 22 motels, many that won the four diamond rating.

He planned a dude ranch and bought 1000 acres in Hernando County. Here he cleared land, created lakes and bridle paths in 783 of the acres he later sold to the state. It has become part of the Withlacoochee State Forest.

Subsequently he relocated to Ellijay, Georgia where he built many homes and town houses as CEO of Ridgehaven Homes. In 2003 he bought Cohutta Lodge which he renovated. The property had 148 acres atop Fort Mountain where he built a Teen Camp and Wilderness Retreat for 400 teens and adults.

Meanwhile the Don CeSar landmark owned by Cigna Insurance Company and later Prudential Insurance Co. had a succession of hotel management companies. There were numerous renovations from 1990 until Loews Hotel Corporation purchased 20 percent of the Don CeSar for allegedly over six times Cigna's original investment.

At this printing Loews Hotels plans to build a state of the arts $8 million Health Spa in 2007.